Little Panda

written by Jay Dale

illustrated by Mélanie Florian

Look at Little Panda!

Little Panda can play.

Little Panda can go
down the hill.

And Little Panda can go
up the hill.

"Mum," said Little Panda.

"Come up here.

Come and play."

"No," said Mother Panda.

"I am down here.

The hill is too big."

11

Little Panda can go down the hill.

Look at Little Panda!

Little Panda can play here.

"Look at me!" said Mother Panda.

"I can play, too!"